Rockets

STAN THE DOG

Stan and the
Major Makeover

STRETCH!

Sco... ...rson

For Ailsa, Emily and Alexander

Rockets series:
CROOK CATCHERS - Karen Wallace & Judy Brown
HAUNTED MOUSE - Dee Shulman
LITTLE T - Frank Rodgers
MOTLEY'S CREW - Margaret Ryan &
Margaret Chamberlain
MR CROC - Frank Rodgers
MRS MAGIC - Wendy Smith
MY FUNNY FAMILY - Colin West
ROVER - Chris Powling & Scoular Anderson
SILLY SAUSAGE - Michaela Morgan & Dee Shulman
SPACE TWINS - Wendy Smith
STAN THE DOG - Scoular Anderson
WIZARD'S BOY - Scoular Anderson

First paperback edition 2003
First published 2002 by A & C Black Publishers Ltd
37 Soho Square, London W1D 3QZ
www.acblack.com

Text and illustrations copyright © 2002 Scoular Anderson

The right of Scoular Anderson to be identified as author
and illustrator of this work has been asserted by him
in accordance with the Copyright, Designs and Patents Act 1988.

ISBN 0-7136-6141-0

A CIP catalogue record for this book is available
from the British Library.

A & C Black uses paper produced with elemental
chlorine-free pulp, harvested from managed sustainable forests.

Printed and bound by G. Z. Printek, Bilbao, Spain.

First Helping

Stan was out in the lane behind his family's house.

He followed the scent.

The bin was outside Fatface's house.
Fatface was a big dog who terrified Stan.

There was no one around.

But the bone
was difficult
to reach...

...and the bin toppled over.

KERRASH!

Stan got his
bone at last
and quickly
headed for
home.

Hope
Fatface
didn't
hear
that!

5

He looked round the corner of the shed
so he could check that none of the
family were watching...

...then he made a dash for the house.

He sneaked in
the back door...

...and into the
sitting room.

He hid the bone in the little cupboard
behind the TV.

Then he went back to his bed and had
a dream about a midnight feast.

Second Helping

Stan woke up when he heard some of
his favourite words.

Let's go out
in the car.

DOG

Stan leapt out of his bed. He didn't want
to be left out of the trip.

STRETCH!

The family got ready. The one Stan called
Crumble packed things into her rucksack.

Handout
pulled things
out of the
hall cupboard.

Bigbelly was
loading the
car.

There was a very tasty smell coming
from the kitchen.

Then Canopener opened a can.

When Stan had gobbled up his lunch,
he had a thought...

He went out
into the hall
and borrowed
a coin from
Handout's
school bus-
money dish.

He flicked the coin in the air.

The family were ready and waiting.

They all went out to the car.

However, no one wanted to sit beside Stan.

At last, Canopener got impatient.

Third Helping

Bigbelly reversed the car out of the drive and off they went. As they reached the end of their street, something caught Stan's eye.

He leapt towards the window.

Crumble was not pleased.

As they reached the end of the next
street, something else caught Stan's eye.

Stan leapt towards the window.

Handout was not pleased.

A little while later, Stan began to feel a bit queasy.

Stan sneaked down onto the floor...

...then, a moment later...

Bigbelly stopped the car and everyone got out. Canopener cleaned up with tissues and wipes.

Everyone was moaning.

At last, they all got back into the car
and drove to a nice spot beside a river.

They all got out.

The family sat down and had their picnic.

Crumble dropped loads of crumbs.

Handout gave Stan a handout.

Bigbelly and Canopener lay down for a snooze while the others went to play.

They ran around in the long grass.

WRUFF!
WRUFF!

Stan found something very smelly to roll in.

This smells nicer than the stuff Bigbelly slaps on his face.

Then they went down to the river.

Handout and Crumble threw stones
into the water.

Stan went to find them.

After that, something caught Stan's eye.
It was a rabbit. He went after it...

...through bracken...

...through brambles...

...into ditches...

...over logs...

...until he was called.

When he came back, no one seemed
pleased to see him.

Stan was
shut in
the car.

The others went for an ice cream in a
nearby cafe. Then they went into a gift
shop. Canopener bought a pair of
Mickey Mouse ears for Crumble...

...and a T-shirt
for Handout.

After that, they got back into the car
and went home.
No one wanted to sit near Stan.

25

Fourth Helping

When they got back home, Stan headed
for the sitting room to check up on his
bone.

He didn't get very far because
Canopener shouted at him.

STAN!

She looked him up and down.

The next morning, Canopener put Stan in the car. She drove to the town centre.

Canopener parked the car outside a shop. It was the...

She was.

Inside the parlour, Stan had to wait in a queue.

At last it
was his turn.
He was
washed.

He had his
nails trimmed.

He had his
teeth brushed.

He had his hair clipped.

30

Canopener even bought him a new collar.

They got back into the car and drove somewhere else.

The dogs and their owners gathered in a field behind the kennels.
Something caught Stan's eye. It was a very familiar face.

As Stan was coming back up the field, he passed Fatface and his owner coming the other way.

Fatface was in a mean mood...

...but Stan's new collar was a bit big so he was able to escape.

He set off down the field.

When he tried to get through the hedge
at the bottom, he got stuck. Canopener
came to rescue him.

She bundled him into the car and took
him home.

Fifth Helping

Next morning, Stan headed for the sitting room to rescue his bone, but something strange was happening.

What are you doing?

Stan's had a makeover – now the sitting room's having one.

It's going to have new paint and wallpaper.

Things were being moved around.

The furniture was covered in sheets.

Ladders and brushes were brought in.

37

Stan began to panic. If he didn't get to his bone soon, someone would find it and he'd be in trouble. When no one was looking he sneaked across the room. He had to climb over a chair to reach the little cupboard.

Then there was a shout from behind him.

He fell off
the chair...

...took the
dustsheet
with him...

...and was banned from the room.

Canopener was ready to start work with her paint scraper.

She opened
a window.

Stan went off to wait for his chance.

Soon he was having a horrible dream.

 Stan was woken up by a noise.

He ran out into the back garden.

He leapt
back into
the house.

He ran as fast as he could through the kitchen.

He walloped right into the washing on the drying stand.

He kept on running even though he
had Handout's new T-shirt wrapped
round his head.

He dived into the sitting room.

He knocked over the stepladder...

...and he got himself wrapped up in dustsheets.

That still didn't stop him.

Fatface had come in through the open window and found the bone but when he saw what was coming towards him...

...he dropped the bone and made a quick exit.

Stan thought he was going to have
another row with Canopener, but he
was wrong.

Canopener stared at the dustsheet then stared at Stan.

She was in such a good mood she let Stan keep the bone to chew in the garden.